For my Michael with love. xx
C. F.

For my mum. I miss you every day! x
A. F.

Text copyright © 2018 by Claire Freedman
Illustrations copyright © 2018 by Alison Friend

First U.S. edition 2019

Library of Congress Catalog Card Number 2018961944
ISBN 978-1-5362-0571-8

19 20 21 22 23 24 TLF 10 9 8 7 6 5 4 3 2 1

Printed in Dongguan, Guangdong, China

This book was typeset in Adobe Caslon.
The illustrations were done in mixed media.

TEMPLAR BOOKS
an imprint of
Candlewick Press
99 Dover Street
Somerville, Massachusetts 02144

www.candlewick.com

BEAR'S BOOK

CLAIRE FREEDMAN   ILLUSTRATED BY ALISON FRIEND

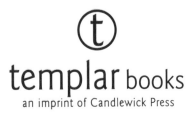

templar books

an imprint of Candlewick Press

Once upon a time, there was a bear
whose favorite thing to do was read.

But Bear had a problem: he had read his book of stories
so many times that it was falling to pieces . . .

and one day a gust of wind blew all the pages away!

Bear decided to make up his own story.
He found a pencil and a notebook, then sat down to write.

All the stories in his old book had exciting beginnings, dramatic middles,
and happy-ever-after endings. But Bear didn't know where to begin his story.
The more he stared at the paper, the more it stared back at him.

Maybe all ideas start with a good back-scratch, he thought.
So he set off to find the perfect tree.

Bear was having a good old scratch when Mouse
came twirling along the blossomy path.

"Hello, Bear!" she called.
"I've got to practice my dancing for the Mouse Ball.
Can you help?"

So Bear whirled and swirled
with Mouse until they were both out of breath.

"Thank you, Bear," said Mouse.
"No problem!" replied Bear.

But Bear did have a problem. Even though he had had
a good back-scratch, he had not thought of a single idea for his story.

Maybe all ideas start with a nice dip in the river, he thought.

Bear was swimming along when he saw Rabbit in her boat.

"Help me, Bear!" she cried. "I've dropped my oars!"

Bear grabbed the boat's towrope and pulled Rabbit to shore.

"Thank you, Bear!" said Rabbit.
"No problem!" replied Bear.

But Bear did have a problem. Even though he had had a swim
and a back-scratch, he still didn't have an idea for his story.

Maybe all good ideas start with tree-climbing, he thought.

Bear found the tallest tree in the forest
and began to climb.

He had almost reached the top when . . .

"Hoot! Hoot! Help!"
came a squeaky little voice.
A baby owl was stuck on a branch and
couldn't get back to his nest.

Bear gently picked him up and put him safely back
with his brother and sister.

"Thank you, Bear!" squeaked the baby owl.
"No problem!" replied Bear.
But Bear did have a problem, because after a back-scratch, a swim,
and a tree-climb, he *still* had absolutely no ideas for his story.

And now his tummy was rumbling.
Time for a snack, he thought, and set off for home.

When he was nice and full, he sat down again to write.
Just then some blossomy petals
floated in through the open window.

They reminded Bear of when he'd danced in the blossoms with Mouse.

Then he remembered rescuing Rabbit and helping the baby owl back to his nest.
Maybe all good ideas start with adventures! he thought.
Bear began to write and draw.

And he didn't stop until the sun went down and his story was finished.
Just then, there was a knock at the door.

Bear's friends were standing on his doorstep with a big basket of berries.
"Thank you for helping us, Bear," they said.
"No!" said Bear. "Thank *you* for giving me ideas for my story!"

"A story! Read it to us! Please, Bear,
please!" they all shouted.

So that's what Bear did.

BEAR'S STORY
by Bear

Once upon a time, a band of pirates set sail, looking for treasure.
The captain was Redbeard Rabbit.
"Arrhh! Shiver me timbers and avast, me hearties!" she roared.

"I like the beginning!" said Rabbit.
"And the middle!" said Mouse.
"And the happy-ever-after ending!" squeaked the baby owls.
They all agreed that it was a very good story.
"Let's have more adventures," they said. "Then Bear can write more stories!"

And that's exactly what they did.